This edition published by Parragon Books Ltd in 2016

Parragon Books Ltd
Chartist House
15–17 Trim Street
Bath BA1 1HA, UK
www.parragon.com

All stories based on the Marvel comic book series *Spider-Man*.

The Last Day of Summer written by Clarissa Wong. Illustrated by Ron Lim and Matt Milla.
Power Trip written by Nancy Lambert. Illustrated by Christian Colbert and Paul Mounts.
Hulk Disposal written by Colin Hosten. Illustrated by Khoi Pham and Matt Milla.
Spider-Man and Nova written by Adam Davis. Illustrated by Ron Lim and Paul Mounts.
Sand Trap written by Colin Hosten. Illustrated by Ron Lim and Matt Milla.
Black Ice written by Nancy Lambert. Illustrated by Christian Colbert and Christopher Sotomayor.
The Amazing Spider-Kid written by Cristina Garces. Illustrated by Khoi Pham and Christopher Sotomayor.
Attack Off Broadway written by Tomas Palacios. Illustrated by Ron Lim and Matt Milla.
Super BUGZ written by Colin Hosten. Illustrated by Khoi Pham and Christopher Sotomayor.
Spider-Man Appreciation Day written by Nancy Lambert. Illustrated by Khoi Pham and Christopher Sotomayor.
Museum Madness written by Andy Schmidt. Illustrated by Khoi Pham and Matt Milla.

ISBN 978-1-4748-3663-0

Printed in China

Storybook
Collection

Bath • New York • Cologne • Melbourne • Delhi
Hong Kong • Shenzhen • Singapore

Contents

The Last Day of Summer

Peter Parker stretched out his arms and leaned back. He was at the beach with his friend Mary Jane, also known as MJ, on the last day of the summer holidays. He was going to make sure it was a blast!

"Ugh, I *can* wait for school to start," MJ grumbled.

"Not now, MJ. Let's enjoy our last day of *freedom*," Peter said.

But MJ continued to whine. "We are going to have to wake up super early to catch the bus, make it through gym class and then come home to a pile of homework!"

That got Peter thinking. Going back to his school, Midtown High, would mean less time as Spider-Man, which was the most amazing part of his life.

Who would want to be Peter Parker when they could be Spider-Man instead? The famous Wall-Crawler could take on the biggest, baddest villains, help others in need, swing from skyscraper to skyscraper through New York City, or just chill out and reflect on life.

"No more hanging out at the beach or staying up late watching TV ..." MJ went on.

"Well, we're still going to stay up late, but working on homework instead," Peter said with a smirk. MJ playfully kicked sand at him.

Suddenly Peter noticed someone he recognized. It was Flash Thompson, a boy from their school.

"Hey, look at that clown!" Flash yelled, laughing and pointing at Peter.

Super Villains, such as Sandman and Doctor Octopus, were meaner than ever before. Spidey barely survived battling them in the summer heat. How was he going to add Flash Thompson to that list now? Flash didn't have super powers, but he did have a way of getting under Peter's skin. Peter had to admit, dealing with a bully – whether human or Super Villain – was tough.

But Peter also had to remember the bigger picture – if they were so set on bringing him down, he must be doing something right ... *right*?

Just then, Peter's spider-sense told him that something was up.

"Hey, twinkle toes! I bet you can't catch this!" Flash yelled as he threw his ball right at Peter's head. Peter knew that with his spider-like reflexes he could easily dodge the football. But then he realized that someone else would get hit. So he let the ball hit him squarely in the head. *THUMP!* Peter's hat flew off and landed in the sand.

Peter took a deep breath as the surrounding children laughed and pointed. He clenched his fists tightly and his face became red with anger. MJ looked frustrated, too. *I have to do something,* Peter thought.

If Peter were Spider-Man right then, he probably could have wrapped Flash in his famous web net, and maybe even dangled the bully over some hungry sharks. Then Peter would have had the last laugh, not Flash Thompson!

He closed his eyes and slowly reminded himself that Peter Parker had powers, too – he could control who annoyed him and who didn't.

Peter let out a sigh and relaxed his fists.

"I guess you're still a bully on your days off, huh, Flash?" MJ shouted.

Peter looked up at MJ. He was surprised to hear his friend stand up to the meanest boy in school. She picked up Flash's ball and threw it into the sea.

"With a friend like you, I'm good," Peter said as he high-fived MJ. In the end, it wasn't so bad to be Peter Parker.

Power Trip

It was the first day of the new term. On the way to school, Peter and his friend MJ were surprised to find the subway closed.

"What happened?" Peter asked a nearby police officer.

"There's been another train accident," the officer said. "The first one happened under the City Art Museum yesterday, and today's was right below Brittany Jewellers."

Hmmm, Peter thought. *Two train accidents in two days? Seems like more than a coincidence. I'd better check it out.*

"I guess we're taking the bus today, Peter," MJ said.

"Actually, you go ahead, MJ. I think I'm going to walk," he replied. Peter waved goodbye and headed to the first crash site.

Peter rushed to the City Art Museum and made his way to the lower level. A massive train carriage was still stuck in the wall where it had crashed earlier. Several museum workers were sifting through the mess.

"Our Michelangelo painting is missing!" said one museum worker. "People are saying the train was haunted. The security cameras prove it. There were no passengers and there was no conductor either!"

Peter wasn't sure about a haunted train, but he was certain those crashes weren't accidents.

Peter headed to the famous Brittany Jewellers next. The owner was very upset.

"The Empire Diamond is missing!" he shouted to the police. "It's one of a kind, worth millions! We've checked every bit of debris, but we can't find it."

"Do you think someone stole it?" an officer asked.

"Maybe...." The owner whispered to the police, "Can I show you something ... odd?"

He pulled out his phone and showed a photo taken by the security camera on the night of the accident.

"At first it just looks like a blast." He zoomed in on the picture. "But look closer, right there – doesn't it look like a man? It's the strangest thing I've ever seen!"

Not that strange, Peter thought, looking at the photo. It was his old nemesis – Electro!

Just then, an emergency call came in on the police officers' radios.

"All units – we have another runaway train," a voice announced.

Time for Spider-Man to get on board, Peter thought as he ducked down the stairs to change into his Super Hero self.

Moments later, Spidey was clinging to the subway ceiling, waiting for the runaway train. He heard the train hurtling towards him. As soon as it started to zoom past, Spider-Man dropped on to its roof.

The Wall-Crawler creeped to the front of the train and peeked over the edge. Just as he expected, Electro was at the controls. Spidey wasn't going to let the electrifying villain get away!

"Don't you need a licence to drive one of these things?" Spidey joked as he smashed through the train's window.

"Don't you just love the subway, Spider-Man?" Electro laughed. "It gets me to all the museums, shops and banks I could ever want ... *to rob*, that is." Electro pushed the throttle lever forwards.

"Let's make this an express." Electro smirked as the train sped down the tracks.

Spidey fired two web lines at Electro, but the villain fried the webbing in mid-air with a burst of lightning. The train went even faster.

"You shouldn't be wasting your time with me, Spider-Man," Electro said with a sneer.

"What do you mean?"

"This train isn't empty like the other ones."

Spidey looked through the conductor's back window. The runaway train was full of terrified people! Electro cackled and pressed the intercom button. "Ladies and gentlemen, the next stop will also be your *last* stop."

Electro zapped the brake system, blowing it out. And just as easily as Spidey had got in, Electro leaped out the broken window and escaped through the electrified rail below the train.

Smoke was coming out of the brake system, and Spidey knew he'd have to stop the train before it crashed.

Good thing I can make my own brakes, he thought. Spidey climbed through the window and quickly shot webbing into the train's many wheels, creating web brakes. Finally, the train began to slow and gradually pulled to a stop. The passengers cheered!

As he helped the passengers safely off the train, Spider-Man wondered what Electro's next target would be. There were hundreds of possibilities along the vast subway system.

Then Spidey glanced at a poster. The National Bank was advertising its new secure vault system. The bank was right above one of the subway lines. Spider-Man remembered Electro mentioning banks in his list of targets.

"Next stop, the National Bank," Spidey said to himself.

A little while later, deep in the vaults of the National Bank, Spidey felt a rumble and suddenly a subway carriage burst through the vault wall.

"Right on schedule," Spidey said when Electro emerged from the dust and smoke.

"I'm not afraid of an itsy-bitsy spider," Electro growled.

He charged at Spidey – but after two lumbering steps, his feet would not budge. He'd walked right into Spider-Man's trap! Spidey tugged hard on the web net he'd set for Electro, pulling him into the air in a bundle of crackling rage.

But Electro wasn't going down without a fight. He ripped out a light fixture nearby, grabbing the sparking wires. He grew brighter as he fully charged. Then he sent a powerful sizzling current of electricity through the web towards Spider-Man!
But with a quick *THWIP*, Spider-Man triggered the sprinkler system and the alarm. Within seconds, Electro's charge fizzled with a hiss.

Just in time, the police came running in with the bank manager.

The next morning, Peter and MJ discovered that the subway entrance was open and the trains were once again safe.

As MJ started to head to the station, Peter paused.

"Wanna walk with me, instead?" Peter asked. "I think I've had enough of trains this week."

MJ smiled, and the two friends made their way to school on foot.

MARVEL
SPIDER-MAN
Hulk Disposal

As well as going to school, Peter Parker worked as a part-time photographer for a newspaper called the *Daily Bugle*. Peter was pretty excited when his boss, John Jonah Jameson, also known as JJ, called him in one day.

"I'm trusting you, Parker," JJ barked, as he handed Peter directions to his next photography assignment. "This job is major!"

Jameson's 'major' assignment was to take pictures for a profile on Mack Scalese, the city's new head of Waste Management. Peter

sighed as he rode his bike to the city dump. It wasn't exactly the exciting job he'd been hoping for.

A large bald man who was wearing a MACK SCALESE name tag called out to Peter from a trailer office. "You must be the kid they sent from the paper," said the man. "Well, come on and take your pictures. I don't have all day."

Peter started
clicking away
on his camera,
but he couldn't
shake the feeling
that something
wasn't right. His
spider-sense was
tingling! But why?
He looked round
and saw a few men
unloading some grey
barrels from a nearby truck.

"Maybe we can get an action
shot over there by those barrels?"
Peter suggested.

"Never mind those barrels!" Mack yelled back. "I think we're done
here. You've got enough pictures."

Peter took one last picture – of the faded symbol on one of the
barrels. He had an idea about what it meant, but he also knew
someone who could say for sure.

Peter took the picture to his friend, the brilliant scientist Dr Bruce Banner. "No doubt about it – that's nuclear waste," Bruce said as he examined the photograph Spider-Man had given him. "This could be very dangerous if not disposed of properly. What are they doing with it at the city dump?"

"Good question," said Peter. "I think I'll go and find out."

"I'll come with you," Bruce said. "We may need to get a sample for testing."

Peter quickly transformed into Spider-Man and used his web-shooters to swing back to the dump with Bruce.

Back at the dump, Spider-Man tried to open a barrel for Bruce.

Just then, a spotlight switched on, dazing them both. Spidey heard a voice that sounded familiar.

"Spider-Man! What are you doing here?" shouted Mack Scalese. "I knew nothing good would come of that reporter. Get rid of them!" he yelled to the dump workers.

Seconds later, Spidey and Bruce fell through a trapdoor. Before Spidey could web his way out of the pit, the steel door slammed shut again. There was no escape!

"It'll take more than that, Mack," Spider-Man said, starting to climb up one of the walls to get to the top. Maybe it was his imagination, but the walls seemed to be moving!

Spidey sighed. It wasn't his imagination. Both walls were moving closer, and Spidey and Bruce were stuck in the middle. They were in a giant rubbish crusher and would be squished into a Spidey and Bruce sandwich in no time!

Spider-Man pushed against one of the walls. It slowed down a little, but it kept closing in. "I hope you're not scared of small spaces," he said, turning to Bruce. "Getting out of this won't be easy."

"I am," said Bruce. "And trust me, it will be."

Suddenly, Spidey noticed that Bruce was turning green – his friend was transforming into the Incredible Hulk!

Back outside, Mack smirked, happy to be rid of Spidey. Suddenly, he heard a loud explosion. He turned round just in time to see the trapdoor flying into the sky, and Spider-Man and a huge green giant emerged from the pit.

"Naughty, naughty, Mack," Spider-Man said, dusting bits of rubbish from his shoulder. "Hulk, do you want to let him know what we do to people who don't recycle?"

"Hulk *SMASH*!"

"Get them!" Mack yelled, waving his hands wildly at his henchmen.

About a dozen men in grey overalls surrounded the Hulk and Spider-Man. One of them kicked over a barrel of nuclear waste in the direction of the Super Heroes.

Spider-Man swung himself up on to a nearby pile of tyres to get out of the way, but Hulk just stood there as the toxic goo flowed over his feet. The nuclear waste had no effect on him. His tough skin made him immune to it. The men gasped and drew back in fear.

"Now you've gone and done it," Spidey said. "He hates getting his feet dirty."

The men tried to turn and run away, but the Hulk had other plans for them. With an incredible roar, the Hulk charged towards the henchmen. It was not going to be a good day for them.

Hulk grabbed the henchmen and threw them into the open rubbish crusher. Once the last one was in, Hulk took a giant piece of scrap metal and slammed it over the opening, trapping them inside.

Meanwhile, Mack was making a break for a rubbish lorry.

Thinking quickly, Spider-Man grabbed an empty barrel and swung it with all his might. The barrel landed directly on top of Mack, who fell over with a crashing *thud*.

"I think it's time to take the rubbish out. What do you say, Hulk?"

"Hulk *TRASH*!"

The next morning, Peter Parker stood in J. Jonah Jameson's office as his boss held up a copy of the *Daily Bugle*.

"The Hulk?" Jameson yelled. "You couldn't even get me one picture of Spider-Man?"

"I'm sorry, JJ. He left too soon. But I'm sure you're happy that we exposed Mack Scalese's illegal dumping operation."

Jameson didn't seem to be listening to him. Peter could still hear him mumbling as he backed out of the office.

"Garbage ... just garbage."

Spider-Man
and Nova

It was a hot summer day. Peter Parker, the amazing Spider-Man, and Sam Alexander, also known as Nova, were in the middle of a friendly but fierce competition to see who was the best Super Hero.

Nova thought he was the best, because he had the ability to fly and release energy pulses. But Spider-Man thought that his agility and web-shooters made him the ultimate Super Hero.

Suddenly, Spider-Man and Nova heard a girl cry for help. They raced to the park.

"What's wrong?" Spidey asked the girl.

"My pet, Vicious, is stuck in that tree," she said.

Spider-Man made a web net and tried to coax Vicious down.

"You're wasting your time, bug breath," Nova shouted, flying up the tree.

Instead of a cat, Nova found a drooling little pug in the tree! Nova was shocked but plucked the dog from the branches.

The little girl was so happy to have Vicious back! She told Nova that he was the best hero she had ever met.

"Looks like I'm winning," Nova bragged to Spider-Man before rocketing into the sky.

"You've just peaked early, helmet head," Spider-Man shot back, webbing his way up a skyscraper.

Spider-Man noticed a long line of angry people by a hot dog stall. "This one's mine!" Spidey shouted to Nova as he swung over. "You need a hand?" he asked the owner of the stall.

"Yeah, I've run out of hot dogs!" the owner replied.

Spider-Man saw a shop nearby and noticed hot dogs on the first shelf. Before Nova could move, Spidey *thwipped* a web into the store and snagged some!

The shop owner looked confused as the hot dogs sped by. Seconds later, another web *thwipped* in with the money to pay for the hot dogs.

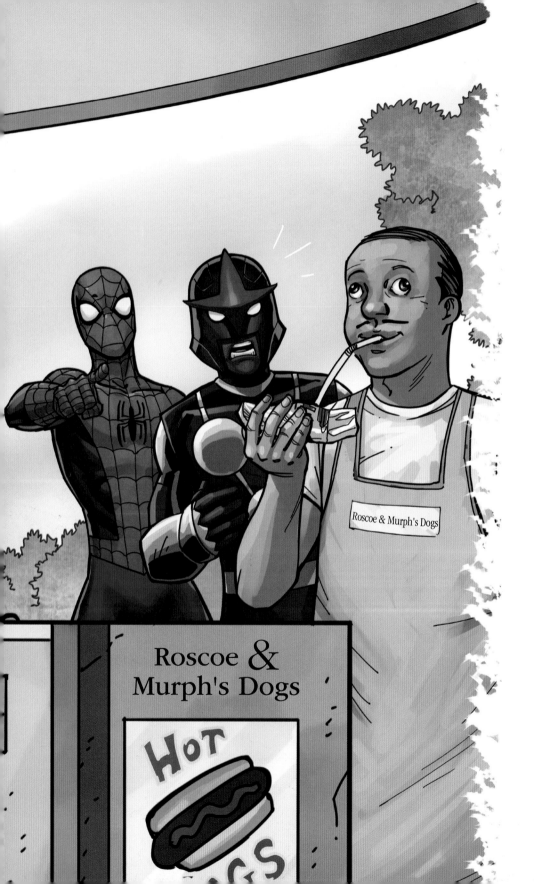

Triumphant, Spider-Man handed the hot dogs to the vendor. But after he dropped them into his cart to cook, the vendor began drinking the hot dog water!

"Ah, nothing like hot dog-flavoured water!" he said.

"Yuck," Nova said.

Spidey shrugged. "But I still won that round."

The heroes needed a tiebreaker. Suddenly, Nova felt a tug on his arm. It was the little girl from the park.

"Excuse me," she squeaked. "Can you help me again?" She pointed up at a towering skyscraper in front of them. Vicious was at the very top!

Nova was shocked. "How did she get up there?"

"She was probably trying to get away from you," Spider-Man teased. "I bet I can rescue her before you!"

"We'll see about that," Nova said as he started to fly.

Spider-Man shot a long web and pulled himself up. The two were neck and neck as they raced up the side of the skyscraper.

Nova edged out in front of Spider-Man, but suddenly the helmeted hero flew into a flock of pigeons. "Ack!" Nova yelled, spitting out feathers. That distraction allowed Spidey to take the lead.

"Looks like this race belongs to me," Spider-Man shouted.

But his lead was short-lived. Both heroes stopped when an explosion rocked the street below! It was Super Villain Doctor Octopus and his Octobot machines. They were trying to destroy a coffee shop.

"Puggly-wuggly's going to have to wait," Spider-Man said.

"We have to get down there!" Nova agreed.

The duo dropped to the ground.

"No one likes decaf!" Dr Ock was yelling. "And your prices are outrageous!"

Spider-Man stepped up. "You leave that shop alone!"

"Or what? You two against my Octobots and me?" Doctor Octopus laughed.

"Let's see how many of those Octobots we can stop," Spider-Man told Nova.

"Now you're on!" Nova yelled.

Spider-Man and Nova jumped into action and began to take out the Octobots. *THWIP! THWACK! KAPOW! KABOOM!*

Nova and Spidey had each destroyed an equal number of Octobots. Doctor Octopus was furious! Finally, he decided to join the fight.

"I'm gonna grind you up and brew both of you!" Dr Ock said with a cackle.

Dr Ock's metal tentacles swung and slashed at the heroes. Spidey leaped and rolled while Nova dived and dodged the attacks.

Working separately, neither hero could grab hold of Dr Ock's tentacles.

"I can't pin down his crazy arms!" Spider-Man yelled to Nova.

"They keep blocking my blasts!" Nova yelled back.

"We have to work together."

Nova grabbed two of Dr Ock's tentacles, and Spider-Man grabbed the other two.

Nova circled Doctor Octopus, wrapping the tentacles round him.

"Let's make it a double knot!" Nova said with a laugh.

Spider-Man swung round Doctor Octopus, mirroring Nova. Then he sealed the tangle of arms with a sticky web.

"All tied up," he joked.

Spider-Man and Nova had destroyed all the Octobots and left Doctor Octopus in a sticky situation. They had learned how important it was to work together, even though their abilities were different. But there was one thing left to do.

"We're still tied," Nova said.

"Who said the competition was over?" Spider-Man shot back.

"Race you to the pug!" they both yelled at the same time, heading to the top of the skyscraper as the little girl watched with a smile.

Sand Trap

A bank alarm wailed loudly as people screamed in fear.

Peter Parker was on his way to the nearby park to take some outdoor spring pictures for the *Daily Bugle* when he heard the alarm and ran towards the bank.

Arriving in front of the bank, he saw a trail of sand disappearing into the entrance and knew exactly who was behind the robbery – Sandman!

Peter looked inside to see the bank vault open and empty.

Looking for a place to change into Spider-Man, Peter spotted the bank manager angrily shaking his head.

"Are you with the newspaper?" the bank manager said, pointing at Peter's camera. "You're too late – he's already gone! You could still take some pictures for the paper, I guess," he said.

"Yeah." Peter sighed, disappointed. "I guess."

Peter was angry with himself for not preventing the robbery. "I could have stopped him if I didn't have to do that story for the *Bugle*," he muttered under his breath.

Frustrated, Peter continued on his way to the park. He snapped some pictures of ducks in the pond, then took one of a tree in full bloom. As he approached the baseball field, he heard shouting.

Peter saw a group of children surrounding a small boy.

"See? That's how you catch a baseball," said one of the children.

"Didn't you ever learn how to catch?" said another.

Peter shook his head. Maybe it was time to remind the children about the importance of playing nice.

"Everything all right here?" he asked as he approached them.

"I wish," replied the tallest, who seemed to be the leader of the pack. "Our team is losing because Ned can't catch a ball!"

Peter knelt down and said, "Ned, is it? I know how you feel – I wasn't that great at catching when I was your age." He turned to the taller boy. "What's your name?"

"Barry," he said, turning his cap round. "I'm the best at baseball!"

"Well, Barry, my name's Peter, and I work for the *Daily Bugle*. I'd love to do a story on the young baseball players we have right here in the park. How about we help Ned become a *better* catcher, instead of making fun of him?"

Barry's eyes glazed over as he pictured himself in the newspaper. "Do you think I could make the front page?" Barry said excitedly.

Peter got his camera ready as the boys took their positions on the field. Ned went to the first base while Barry covered the second.

"Okay," Peter yelled, "let's see what you've got!"

One boy threw the ball and the batter swung hard, sending the ball flying. Diving at full stretch to his left, Barry scooped the ball off the ground and jumped to his feet to throw the ball to first base.

Ned was only a few metres away, at first base. All Barry had to do was throw the ball over to him and the batter would be out. Instead, he reared back his arm and rocketed the ball at Ned, who ducked out of the way just in time to avoid getting hit in the face! The ball went rolling away, and the batter safely went past first base and headed to second.

"You let him get to second base!" Barry yelled angrily at Ned.

"Wait a minute. That's not fair," Peter called out. "You threw that too hard for him to catch!"

Barry laughed. "He would've dropped it even if I'd handed it to him!"

Just then, out of the corner of his eye, Peter saw the sand on the pitch moving.

That's strange, he thought. A second later, it got even stranger – the sand started rising, and a face took shape. It was Sandman!

"You're stomping all over my getaway hideout!" the villain yelled.

"Run!" Barry shouted at the top of his voice, and disappeared behind a tree. Most of the other boys followed him – but Ned stood still, too scared to move.

Peter knew he had to do something, but there was no time to change into Spider-Man. He had to distract Sandman somehow.

"Hey, look over here!" Peter cried as he clicked away with his camera.

"Oh, good, the media." Sandman loved being the centre of attention. "I always wanted to be the most famous Super Villain in the world."

It was working! Peter just had to work out what to do next. He saw a fountain in the park and quickly came up with a plan.

"Barry," Peter cried, "throw the ball at the bag of money!"

Barry gripped the ball. "I can't get the right angle!"

"Then throw it to Ned!" Peter yelled. "Remember – throw it so he can *catch* it!" Peter said to Barry. Barry nodded, then threw the ball to Ned. Ned caught it!

"Okay, Ned," Peter called, "throw it at the bag of money – now!"

Ned took aim and threw the ball with all his might. He hit Sandman right in the wrist, and the thief dropped the bag!

Then it was Peter's turn. While everyone was looking at Sandman, Peter quickly shot a strand of webbing at the fountain, then pulled back sharply. The fountain fell right off its base and shot a spray of water into the air, right at Sandman!

"Noooo!" Sandman cried, turning into a muddy puddle.

"Wow, Ned, that was a great throw!" Barry went over and gave Ned a high five. "I didn't know you had it in you."

"I didn't, either," said Ned, looking up and smiling at Peter. "Thanks!"

"We should all be thanking *you*, Ned," said Peter. "Now, let's take that front-page picture."

Black Ice

It was a bright winter morning when the students of Midtown High arrived at the Empire Mountain Ski Resort for their winter school trip. Peter was looking forward to having fun with his friends and maybe learning how to snowboard.

But just as the students were checking in, they heard a low, distant rumble.

"Avalanche!" shouted one of the ski instructors. Everyone ran inside the lodge, but Peter ducked behind a rack of skis. It was time for Spidey to hit the slopes.

From the lodge roof, Spider-Man saw the avalanche tumbling towards the resort. There had to be a way to keep the crushing wall of snow from hitting the lodge!

Spidey looked round and saw snow piled against some orange plastic safety nets that lined the beginner slopes.

My webs may not be orange, he thought, *but they'll do the trick.*

He worked quickly, attaching several large webs to the steel ski-lift poles that ran past the lodge. The avalanche roared down the mountain, faster than a speeding car. Spidey braced himself for the impact, but it never came. The nets had worked!

Just then, Spidey noticed a black shadow flicker in the corner of his eye. It was Venom! Venom was an alien made out of a gooey black suit that gave him powers just like Spider-Man's ... and more. He was obsessed with crushing the Wall-Crawler.

Venom skulked along the ski-lift cables. The lift was empty because of the avalanche warning, but Spider-Man knew he still had to lure Venom away from the lodge. Spidey swung up to the ski lift and landed on the side that moved up the mountain.

"Look who it is," Spidey said, "my number-one stalker. What are you doing here?"

"Spider-Man," Venom hissed, slinking over to join Spidey on the uphill lift. "I'm just here for the snow. What better place to hang out than a ski lodge? You know I don't care for hot weather...." He grinned, lashing his long tongue in the air. One of Venom's few weaknesses was extreme heat.

Before Spidey could make a plan, Venom charged at him.

They were only a few metres away from the loop at the top of the ski lift. Soon they'd be heading back down the mountain, towards the lodge and the students. Spidey had to stop the lift – and fast! Instead of firing his webs at Venom, Spider-Man blasted two thick coils of web into the gears of the lift. The gears stuck. The engine creaked and groaned and shook – and then, finally, it jolted to a halt with a loud *BANG!* Spider-Man and Venom flew into the empty lift station, crashing through it just as the cables snapped!

Spider-Man pushed himself up a split second before Venom's fist pounded into the snow right where Spidey's head had been. Spidey grabbed a pipe from the wreckage to block Venom. *WHAM!* The pipe bent with the force of Venom's blow, but Spider-Man smacked it into Venom's chest. It stuck in Venom's tar-like suit!

"If only I'd packed a flamethrower," Spidey grumbled as Venom grabbed a bright-red rescue vehicle and smashed it at the Web-Slinger's feet. *That's it!* Spidey thought. The rescue cabin at the bottom of the black diamond trail had an emergency warming shelter – with blazing-hot lamps ready at the flip of a switch.

Those lamps should give off enough heat to stop Venom, Spidey thought. *But first I've got to get there.*

Spider-Man snatched a long broken board and jumped on to it. *I guess I'm learning how to snowboard now!* he thought, speeding down the steep black diamond trail.

Venom screeched and ran after Spidey. But with his makeshift snowboard, Spider-Man was faster. Suddenly, Venom stopped. Spidey skidded to a halt and glanced behind him, worried that Venom was going to race back to the lodge. But Venom just stood there and grinned.

Venom tilted back his oily head, opened his vicious mouth wide, and gave a mighty roar. The sound echoed off the mountains around them. The ground began to shake and rumble. Venom had triggered another avalanche!

Venom cackled as he grabbed a broken board for himself and rode the churning waves of snow towards Spider-Man.

Venom shot sticky patches of thick black webbing at Spidey, who swerved to avoid being hit. The rescue cabin was close. But Venom was gaining on Spidey – fast. It was now or never. As Spidey leaped off his board, he shot two bolts of webbing into the snow, creating a huge mound. Spider-Man tumbled to a halt right by the cabin and scrambled to his feet.

Venom flew up Spidey's snow ramp and sailed over Spider-Man's head, hissing viciously as he went by. He landed in a deep drift beside the cabin. The avalanche tumbled past. Spidey yanked the warming-station switch just as Venom exploded from the snowdrift.

"Spider-Man, you've run out of mountain ... and time." Venom hurtled towards Spidey.

He didn't notice the heat-lamp coils turning bright red over Spider-Man's head. *It's not heating fast enough!* Spidey thought as Venom closed in on him. Just then, Spidey heard a loud hiss. This time it wasn't Venom – it was the snow melting under the powerful lamps. Venom heard the hiss, too. He looked up, but it was too late. He gave one last roar as he began to melt away with the ice.

Spidey was happy to be rid of Venom! He hurried back to the lodge to change into his normal Peter Parker clothes before a crowd could gather.

Later, MJ joined Peter by the fire in the lodge. "It's a shame about the broken lift, huh?" she said.

"I'm just happy to be inside, where it's warm." Peter smiled. "And safe!"

The Amazing Spider-Kid

Zack lived with his brother, Jake, and his parents in a small town, and he loved Spider-Man. In fact, Spider-Man was his favourite Super Hero! Zack wore pyjamas that made him look just like the famous Wall-Crawler. Every night, as he drifted off to sleep, Zack imagined what it would be like to fight bad guys alongside his idol.

One Friday, as Zack was walking home from school, he felt a little tingle on his arm. *What was that?* he thought.

He looked down in time to see a small spider scurrying away. He scratched at his arm and suddenly felt a surge of energy. *Was it a spider bite?* Zack thought.

The next morning, he went downstairs and told his family about it.

"Think fast!" Jake yelled, and threw an orange right at Zack's head. Zack quickly caught it, surprising everyone.

"Whoa!" Jake cried. "Rumour has it Spider-Man got his powers because he was bitten by a radioactive spider. What if it's happening to you, too?"

Am I turning into ... Spider-Kid? Zack wondered. *I need to test this out.* Zack finished his breakfast, put on his Spider-Man costume and packed his Spider-Man boots in his rucksack. Then he set off to test his new-found powers.

Zack rode his bike down the street before he noticed his classmate, Anna, sitting on her porch. She looked upset.

"My spider-sense is tingling!" he said to himself as he rode up to Anna's steps.

"What's wrong?" Zack asked.

"I was playing with my dog, Chewie, and he saw a squirrel and ran away! Can you help me find him?" Anna said.

What would Spider-Man do? Zack thought. He scanned the garden and noticed paw prints leading to a bush.

"Aha!" he yelled. The bush had thorns, so he carefully parted the branches. There was Chewie!

"Oh, Zack, thank you!" Anna cried. "You're my hero!"

"All in a day's work," Zack said, and he got back on his bike and rode off in search of another adventure.

Let's see what other powers I have, Zack thought. He continued riding and found his friend Gerald on the kerb beside a bike.

"Zack!" Gerald yelled. "I was just riding my brother's bike, and the chain fell off into this ditch. Can you help me reach it? He's going to be so upset if I bring it back broken."

"This looks like a job for Spider-Kid!" Zack said.

Zack noticed a muddy ledge that led down the wall of the ditch. He put on the boots of his Spider-Man costume. He didn't want his mum to get angry with him for getting his shoes dirty again.

"There!" Zack said excitedly. He found the bike chain and took it back to Gerald.

"You saved the day!" Gerald shouted.

"Maybe I *am* Spider-Kid," Zack said to himself. "I can do anything Spider-Man can!" he yelled as he sped down the street on his bike, proud of his new powers. Suddenly, he ran straight into a set of long metal legs and fell off his bike.

It was Doctor Octopus, fleeing from a bank robbery! Zack was afraid, and he thought of running away. Dr Ock was a real villain. Could Zack stand up to him? *But Spider-Man would be brave,* Zack thought.

"Stop there! You shouldn't steal. I'm not afraid of you!" he shouted at Dr Ock.

"Why, you are just a little boy!" Doctor Octopus mocked.

"I'm Spider-Kid, and you better watch out!" Zack responded.

Dr Ock grinned and said, "What could you possibly do to hurt me?"

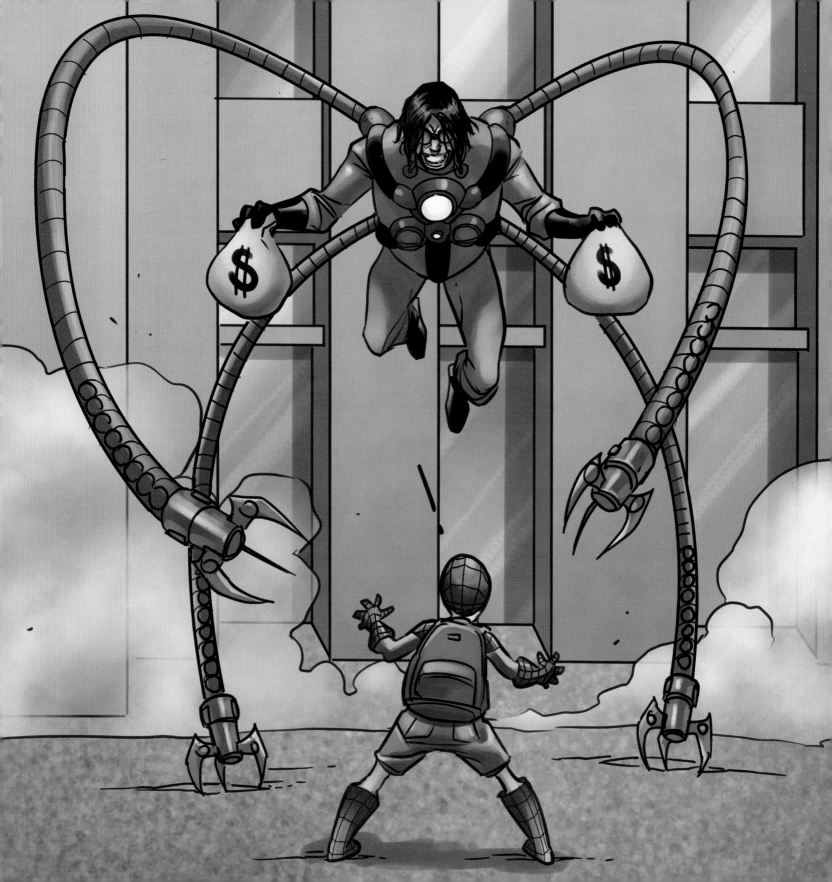

How would Spidey get out of this? Zack thought. "Yes!" he cried, getting an idea. "I've got something up my sleeve." He stuck out his arms. "One ... two ... three!" Zack closed his eyes and willed himself with all his might to shoot webs from his hands, just like Spider-Man! He opened one eye – nothing had happened. "One more try," Zack whispered in a panic, and then he shut his eyes and tried again.

"*Aaarrghhhh!*" Dr Ock cried.

Zack opened his eyes. Dr Ock was covered in webs! Zack stared down at his palms in wonder. He closed his eyes and thrust his hands out again. *Thwip-thwip! Thwip-thwip!* With each *thwip*, one of Dr Ock's tentacles was covered in webbing.

Then Zack heard a voice from behind him. "Looks like you need a hand ... or eight." It was the *real* Spider-Man!

"Nothing can stop me!" Dr Ock yelled, breaking the webs.

"Come on, Spider-Kid, we can handle this one together," Spider-Man said. Zack beamed. He was finally fighting crime with his favourite Super Hero.

"I'll distract him," Zack said excitedly.

"I like your style, Spidey-Kid. Let's go!" said Spider-Man.

Zack jumped in front of Dr Ock. "Hey, spaghetti arms! I bet you can't catch me!" He hopped on his bike and pedalled as fast as he could. The villain followed angrily.

Just as Dr Ock started gaining on Zack, Spider-Man swooped in.

Spidey used his webs to tie up Dr Ock.

"You did it!" Zack cried. "You saved the day!"

"*We* did it," Spider-Man replied. He knelt down next to Zack. "You did a great job today. You learned that there's a Super Hero in all of us," he added. "But sometimes even Super Heroes need help. And that's okay."

"Thanks, Spidey," Zack said.

Later that night, Zack thought about his day's adventures. The night before, he had only dreamed of fighting the bad guys with Spider-Man. That day, his dream had come true!
"It's tough being a Super Hero," he said, sighing.
Zack climbed into bed and began to dream about his next adventure with his hero Spider-Man.

Attack Off Broadway
Guest Starring Rocket and Groot

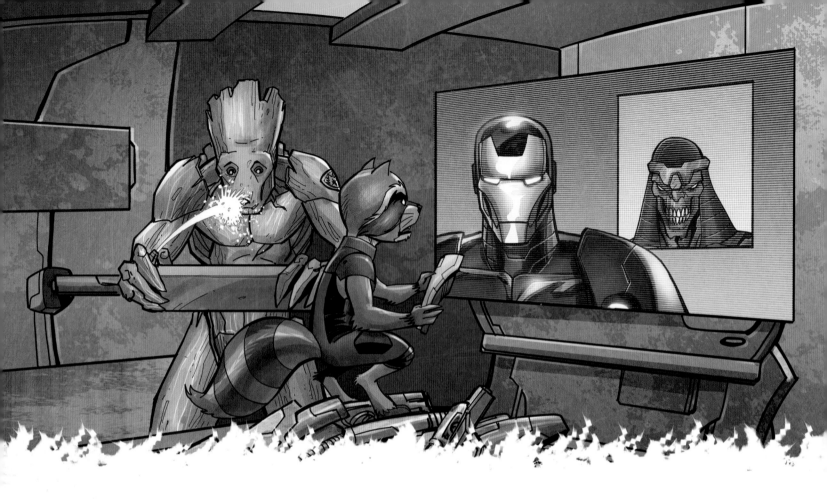

After fighting giant space piranhas all weekend, Super Heroes Rocket Raccoon and Groot needed a holiday. Suddenly their friend Iron Man appeared on their telemonitor.

"I need help. A Chitauri space pirate is causing mischief in New York. I need you to stop him!"

Groot smiled and said "I am Groot" – the only three words he could say!

"He means we'd love to help," Rocket explained.

Rocket pointed their spaceship towards Earth and they blasted off.

They landed in Times Square, parked their ship and left the key with a parking attendant for safe-keeping.

Rocket climbed Groot's branches and leaned out in excitement. "Times Square! The centre of the universe! The city that never sleeps! The Big Apple!"

Groot frowned. "I am Groot!"

"Don't worry. I won't eat it," replied Rocket.

"Now, if I was a Chitauri space pirate, where would I be?" asked Rocket.

"*Wow!* Look at those costumes!" came a voice from above them.

They turned and saw a friendly neighbourhood Super Hero swinging down to meet them.

"I am Groot!" Groot said, recognizing their old friend.

"And I'm Spider-Man!"

Rocket sighed. "That's what Groot *just said*."

"It sounded like he said, 'I am Groot,'" Spidey replied.

"He did, but ... never mind. Listen, we need help finding a Chitauri space pirate. He's out here somewhere in New York, and we need to stop him before he causes havoc."

Spidey nodded. "Okay, wait a minute. *Where* did you get these costumes?" He tugged at Rocket's whiskers. "They seem so real! Like, the *real* Rocket Raccoon real!"

"I *am* Rocket Raccoon."

"Whoa!" Spidey cried. "Rocket! Groot! Long time no see!"

But before the friends could catch up, screams rang out from a nearby street. The Chitauri villain was about to destroy a street-performing Iron Man. "He thinks that's the *real* Iron Man!" Spider-Man said.

The three heroes jumped into action! Spidey swung towards the Chitauri and blasted him with webbing. Groot charged forwards with battle-ready fists. And Rocket ... well, Rocket ate a New York City hot dog. His mission was complete ... or so he thought!

"He's heading towards a theatre!" Rocket cried.

"Let's cut him off," Spider-Man replied. "Follow me."

The three raced down an alley and through a door. Suddenly, they were onstage in a Broadway play! The Chitauri fired a blast from his plasma cannon at Groot and Spidey, then ran offstage. Rocket paused to bow to the crowd as he received a standing ovation.

The Super Heroes chased the Chitauri into the subway.

They jumped into the train as dozens of people scattered and ducked for cover. Groot politely nudged the passengers to one side to protect them as Rocket aimed his laser cannon at the Chitauri.

"No drinking, no eating and *no* radioactive weapons on the train, dude!" Spidey said.

"Oh, *fine*," Rocket replied as the train stopped and the Chitauri jumped out. "But he's getting away!"

The Chitauri raced up the steps to the surface, and everyone scrambled in panic as he blasted his plasma cannon.

By the time Spidey, Rocket and Groot got back to street level, it was a sea of running people. They had lost the Chitauri! But then something caught Groot's eye.

"I ... am ... Groot?" he said, pointing to a giant shop window. On display was a beach scene with all the trimmings – a mannequin lifeguard, some beach balls, towels, mannequin children playing, mannequin parents watching – and a Chitauri in sunglasses.

Spidey shrugged. "I'd say that's weird, but we are in New York City...."

"Enough!" Spidey added. "We've been through Times Square, a theatre, the subway, a window display ..."

"And a hot dog stand," Rocket said. "Don't forget that."

"Let's end this now!" Spidey said. "Here's the plan – I wrap him up, Groot knocks him out and then Rocket takes him down. Ready?"

"I *am* Groot!"

"I totally agree!" Spidey replied.

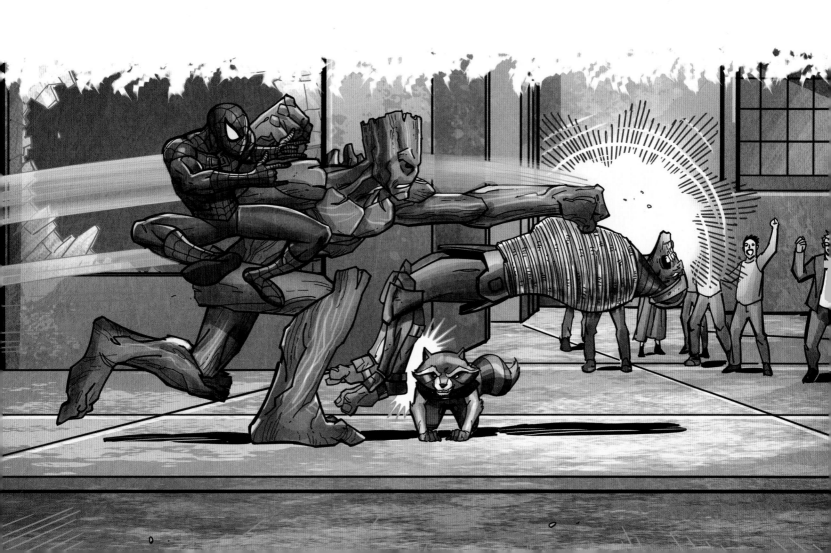

Once the Chitauri was defeated, Spidey helped load the space pirate on to Rocket and Groot's ship and the parking attendant gave the key back to Rocket.

Spidey suddenly had a thought. "Wait, guys! We need some photos!"

"I am Groot?"

"Yes, we can get pics of the Statue of Liberty, Central Park, and the Bronx Zoo," Spidey replied.

"That's not what he said," Rocket replied.

"I know," Spidey said. "But I'm getting close."

"Nowhere near," sighed Rocket.

MARVEL
SPIDER-MAN
Super BUGZ

Spider-Man groaned in frustration as the computer locked him out for the seventh time. He'd just caught the criminal Alexander Petrovski hacking into the secured network of the First National Bank. Now Spider-Man was trying to reverse Petrovski's work. But he wasn't having much luck.

"Maybe I could give you a hand with that?"

Spider-Man looked round, startled, but Petrovski's mouth was covered – and there was no one else in the room.

Spidey looked down but still saw nothing.

"Hold on," someone said.

A moment later, a man was standing in front of Spidey.

"Ant-Man!" Spidey exclaimed. "You certainly know how to make an entrance. What are you doing here?"

"Same thing you are," Ant-Man replied, pointing over to Petrovski. "I've been tracking him for weeks now."

"Really?" Spidey said. "I just happened to be passing by a cybercafe when my spidey-sense started tingling. Petrovski ran off, and I followed him to this warehouse."

"Spidey-sense, huh? Must be nice."

"Oh, it's great, but it doesn't work for guessing passwords."

"Just leave that to me," Ant-Man said, shrinking and disappearing through the side of the computer.

"It should be a piece of cake," he called from inside. "Just push this wire here, press that switch there and *presto*!" A few seconds later, Ant-Man was standing next to him again.

"Great work!" Spider-Man said. "You just saved thousands of people a lot of money."

"Correction, Spidey – *we* just saved them a lot of money."

"Wait a minute," Spidey said. "Are you thinking what I'm thinking?"

Ant-Man stroked his chin and nodded. "Your spidey-sense, my shrinking ability ..."

"We could be –"

"– the SUPER BUGZ!"

"Hold on, though," Spidey said. "I don't know if my spidey-sense still works if I'm ant-sized."

"Only one way to find out," Ant-Man replied. "Let's test it!"

They left Petrovski tied up for the cops and went outside. Ant-Man sprayed Peter with his special shrinking particles.

Suddenly, they were both looking up at pieces of rubbish towering above them on the pavement.

"It worked!" Spidey cheered, looking up at the warehouse that now seemed like a skyscraper.

"Do you feel any different?" Ant-Man asked.

"A little hungry, but I skipped lunch. I think my spidey-sense still works – it's even tingling right now!"

"What? Right now?"

"Yes! Return us to normal size, quick!"

Ant-Man pressed a button on his belt to spray the particles, but nothing happened. "Uh-oh."

"Let me guess," Spidey groaned. "It has a bug?"

Ant-Man nodded. "I can fix it, but I need a few minutes."

"I'm not sure we have that long," Spidey said, pointing to a pigeon that had landed a few metres away. It was only a regular bird, but it looked like a winged dinosaur to the tiny Spider-Man and Ant-Man. A hungry bird of prey coming right for them!

Spidey and Ant-Man jumped away just as the pigeon's beak snapped at them.

"I'll hold it off!" Spidey yelled. "You fix the belt!"

The bird flapped its wings and dived at them again. Quickly, Spidey shot a burst of webbing and hoisted himself on to the pigeon's back.

"Hey, this isn't so bad," he said. "It's a bit like a ride at the fair!"

Just then, the bird reared back and shot straight into the air. "Whoa!" Spidey shouted. "How do you get off this ride?"

Spidey held tightly as the pigeon zipped under, over and around. He wasn't afraid of heights, but then he'd never ridden on the back of a bird before. He hoped Ant-Man was close to fixing the device.

"Uh, one little problem ... I can't spray you when you're so far away!" Ant-Man explained.

"Throw the belt to me! I'll catch it!" Spidey shouted.

"Are you sure? I don't want the bird to eat it...."

"Just do it!" Spidey yelled.

Ant-Man shouted, "Hey, birdie! Down here!" The pigeon suddenly dived, speeding towards the pavement.

"Anytime you're ready, Ant-Man!" Spider-Man yelled.

"Get ready!" Ant-Man held up the belt. Without a moment to lose, Spidey aimed his web-shooter. It was his only chance!

"Here goes nothing," the Wall-Crawler whispered to himself. He snatched the belt seconds before the pigeon could!

Spidey sprayed himself with the shrinking particles and tumbled to the ground.

The world seemed to spin, and then he was on the pavement looking down at Ant-Man.

Ant-Man laughed. "Do you know what? Maybe that whole Super BUGZ idea needs a little more work."

Spidey chuckled with him. "We do make a good team, but I prefer to fly without a co-pilot – especially one with bird brains!"

Spider-Man Appreciation Day

"Whoa." Peter stopped in front of the Spider-Man Appreciation Day Festival. He smiled when he saw all the Spider-Fan gear. There were signs and banners everywhere! Some read 'THANK YOU, SPIDER-MAN!' and others said 'WE LOVE YOU, SPIDEY!' By the looks of it, everyone in New York City was there to celebrate.

But Peter knew at least one person who would not be attending: J. Jonah Jameson, Peter's boss at the *Daily Bugle*. JJ held a grudge against the famous Web-Slinger, and wanted to convince the city that Spider-Man was a menace. He had assigned Peter to take a few photos of the festival – but only so he could make fun of the hero in the next day's paper.

After snapping some shots, Peter looked for a place to change into the hero of the hour. He saw some men handing out rubber Spidey masks.

"Here," said one of the men, offering Peter a mask.

"No, thanks. I, uh, brought my own," Peter replied with a smirk.

"Just *take* it," the man hissed through gritted teeth, shoving it into Peter's hand. "Put it on before Spider-Man gets here."

But Peter tossed it in a rubbish bin as the man walked away.

At first Peter wasn't sure whether the sudden edginess he felt was his spider-sense tingling or just nerves about his upcoming speech. But when he got onstage as Spider-Man, he realized it was definitely his spidey-sense. The festival was in chaos!

The fans who had been celebrating moments earlier were rampaging! They knocked down food stalls, and they trashed banners and displays.

I was expecting Spider-Fans, not Spider-Foes! the Web-Slinger thought as he glanced around. Then he noticed something even stranger about the suddenly angry crowd – every single one of them was wearing a Spider-Man mask! Before he could work out what was happening, he heard a familiar voice behind him.

"How quickly they turn, eh?" Doctor Octopus said as he stepped out from behind the curtains on the stage.

"I thought something was fishy," Spidey said, waving his hand in front of his face. "I didn't know it was an octopus I smelled."

"Sorry to crash your party." Dr Ock laughed. "Actually, no, I'm not. This is the only way I could be sure you wouldn't interfere."

The Super Villain punched a few buttons on a controller wrapped round one of his tentacles. The device flashed, and everyone in the crowd roared at once. They all charged the stage. "Sorry, Spidey – looks like your 15 minutes of fame are up."

As Dr Ock lumbered towards the nearby Research Centre, the crowd of masked Spider-Foes swarmed the real Spidey.

Trying not to hurt anyone, Spidey shot a web towards the rafters above the stage and pulled himself free. But the moment he landed, another group of Spider-Foes began to chase him.

Spidey quickly ducked round a corner. There seemed to be nowhere to hide. *Except in plain sight,* he thought. Spidey pressed up against a life-size poster of himself, striking the same wall-crawling pose. The Spider-Foes ran right past him!

With a quick *thwip*, Spidey pulled a mask from a nearby boy and examined it. The boy looked bewildered.

"Ha! Mind-control sensors – knew it," Spider-Man said, pulling a small, round electrical node from the mask.

"Spider-Man?" The kid rubbed his unbelieving eyes. "Whoa. Spider ... everyone?"

"Somehow, Dr Ock is controlling the people with these masks," Spidey said. "I have to stop him. But first I need to do something about these Spider-Shams."

Spidey tried to remove the masks from as many people as he could. He shot webs left and right, all the while dodging capture. But there were just too many of them! He crouched behind a snack stand. "I'll be here all day if I try to do it this way," Spidey said, watching an abandoned candyfloss machine spin a pink ball of fluffy sugar. Suddenly, he had an idea!

Spider-Man jumped on to the candyfloss machine. He balanced carefully on its rotating centre and began to spin rapidly with it. Spidey pointed his web-shooters at the crowd.

"This round is on me!" he shouted. While the machine spun him round and round, Spider-Man was able to cover the crowd quickly with a thick net of webbing, trapping them. *THWIP-THWIP! THWIP! THWIP!* "That should keep them busy for a while," he said, jumping off the spinner. "Now, let's see what Dr Ock is up to."

When Spidey entered the nanotech labs, he found Ock tapping furiously on a computer keyboard. His masked minions surrounded him.

"Once I've hacked into this system, I'll have the technology I need to bring my mind-control powers to the entire city!"

"No way, Doc," Spider-Man said as he shot his webbing at the villain – but the minions blocked the webs!

"You're right!" Dr Ock laughed. "Why stop at the city? With my mind-control nodes, I can play everyone in *the whole world* like a deck of wild cards."

"You wouldn't want to hurt your supporters," Dr Ock added, pressing a button. The minions protecting him regained control of their minds.

"Spider-Man! Help!" they shouted. Dr Ock pressed the button again, and they fell silent.

"Time to meet your fans!" he cackled.

"Let me roll out the *web carpet* for them," Spidey said. He shot a thick layer of webbing at the minions' feet.

Dr Ock growled and reached for Spider-Man with his tentacles.

With a *thwip*, Spidey ripped a cluster of electrical wires from one of the computers and smacked it into Dr Ock's metallic arm! The mind controller fell from his tentacle and slid across the floor, stopping at Spider-Man's foot.

With a mighty stomp, Spidey crushed the controller. The minions returned to normal and began taking off their masks.

Spidey had saved the day!

The next morning, Peter wasn't surprised to see the headline on the front page of the *Daily Bugle* – 'SPIDER-SCAM!!!'

"I guess Spider-Man Appreciation Day won't be an annual event," Peter said, sighing.

Museum Madness

On a school trip to New York City's world-famous Metropolitan Museum of Art, Peter Parker and Mary Jane were having two very different experiences.

Peter was thrilled to see ancient artefacts such as the mummies, the knights in shining armour, the sword-wielding samurai, and the ancient Greek heroes of old, including Hercules! MJ was not as impressed.

"These things are *soooo* 3000 years ago," she said.

"That's exactly right, MJ," Peter replied excitedly. "That's what makes them so amazing! Most of these heroes didn't have super powers, which means that any one of us could be a hero!"

As Peter went on about the ancient Greeks, MJ noticed a strange mist coming out of the museum floor.

But neither of them noticed that the statues were coming to life!

Just in time, Peter's spider-sense began to tingle.

The statues started grabbing Peter's classmates. A Japanese samurai warrior and an Egyptian mummy caught Dylan and Sofia. Across the room, a medieval knight snatched Owen.

When MJ turned to check on Peter, he was gone! She ran to find help.

While MJ was distracted by the museum madness, Peter had run into one of the smoke clouds and changed clothes. He came out of the other side as SPIDER-MAN!

"Hey! How exactly *did* you guys just come to life?" Spidey asked the statues. "Was it magic?"

"Spider-Man! Help us!" cried Dylan. The heroic Wall-Crawler knew the first thing he had to do was get his classmates to safety.

Careful not to harm any of the living artefacts, the web-slinger snatched his classmates and dropped them on to a giant web.

"Hey, Spidey!" Sofia called. "Did you see that samurai?"

Spider-Man looked back and saw that the samurai had sprouted wiring. "There must be a robot underneath his armour!" Spider-Man exclaimed.

"You may be covered in history, but you're just metal and wires underneath," Spidey said as the statues closed in on him. "Catch me if you can!" He quickly created a shield of webbing that would help protect the artefacts ... and himself!

Spidey raised his cushiony shield and spun a web round all the statues' feet! "I'd better move fast! My shield will only last so long," Spidey said.

Just before the knight's sword could rip through his shield, Spider-Man webbed his last opponent's legs!

With all his spider might, the Wall-Crawler leaped into the air, holding tightly to the web.

The higher he rose, the more his web tightened, pulling and dragging the statues together by their ankles!

"Why don't you fellas hang out for a bit while I get to the bottom of this mystery?" Spidey said.

"Look no further, Spider-Man!" Spidey turned to see Mysterio – master of illusion – coming out of the smoke. "You've stopped my robots for the last time. Let us finish this game, Web-Slinger!"

"Now you'll battle my masterpiece – the Sphinx!" added Mysterio.

As the Sphinx came to life, Spidey saw that MJ was back – and she'd brought the police with her!

Spider-Man struggled with all his might against the Sphinx, barely able to hold it over his shoulders.

Mustering all his strength, Spider-Man gave the Sphinx one last push and hurled it away!

"No matter," Mysterio said as MJ snuck up behind him with Hercules's heavy mace.

"Do you *ever* stop talking?" MJ asked as she struck Mysterio over the head. *SMASH!* "You sound like Peter Parker!"

The police entered the scene and quicky handcuffed the villain.

Spider-Man sheepishly approached MJ. "Thanks for your help," he said, trying not to sound too much like Peter.

"A friend told me you don't need super powers to be a hero," MJ replied, smiling.